The Summer House

The First Summer

by Rosalie Intartaglia

Dedicated to my parents,

Dominick and Lillian Intartaglia,

my brother Michael, and

my sister Andréa.

Thank you for my life.

With God all things are possible.

CONTENTS

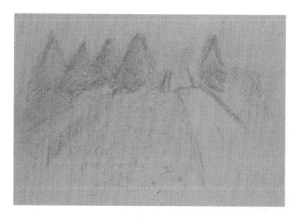

FINDING HOME

They weren't in Brooklyn anymore. It was the spring of 1972. Mom and Dad thought it would be a good idea if they spent summers somewhere other than Brooklyn. Rosalie and her brother, Michael were in the back seat of their car watching the tall buildings of the city slowly getting replaced with trees and mountains. The streets turned into long winding roads. Mountains covered in shades of green surrounded them. Looking to the left and right of the never ending mountains, the sky seemed bluer. The world she knew was disappearing through the rear view window of their car. Rosalie fell asleep somewhere along Route 17 and woke up in Oneonta, New York, in the parking lot of the Oasis Motel. There was an immense illuminated sign of a smiling child swinging on a swing. Oneonta did not look like the country, but it wasn't the suburbs of Brooklyn either. She was tired and Dad carried her to their hotel room. With her head resting on his warm shoulders she saw Mom right behind them with Michael cradled in her arms.

They woke up the next morning to meet the realtor. She showed them several houses and then they drove to South New Berlin, about 30 minutes from where they were staying. The road winded left and right, up and down. There were no signs of a town anywhere and Oneonta seemed as foreign as Brooklyn now. They passed farms where cows were outside eating grass, scattered in the fields. Chickens were walking freely outside, pecking at the ground. Rosalie saw horses with tails swooshing the flies away. Some had foals standing next to them. A mare protectively looked around and then gently gave her baby a reassuring touch of her nose. She had never seen anything more beautiful, more peaceful.

They came upon a house sitting far back from the road. It had a circular driveway, a slate front porch, and the windows on the side of the house looked like smiling eyebrows. The house was red and white with a green roof. Lush grass was everywhere and the fields and mountains across the road never seemed to end. Birds flew through the air circling above them. It was so peaceful there.

The house had two entrances. One large grand door in the middle of the house and one entrance to the left by a screened in porch. The mailbox read "Aiders – R. D. 1 Box 146". There was a detached pale green garage by the left side of the driveway, right by the road, perfect for horses she thought. She knew she was home.

"There's a side porch entry way to the left. We'll go in that way," said the realtor. They saw a red water pump in the middle of the lawn in front of the left side of the house. "The water pump works, by the way," said the realtor as if she knew what they were thinking. They walked up the four steps and through a screen door that led them onto the large front porch lined with windows. In front of them was a massive white wooden door. It was beautifully carved and had a window half the size of the door. An old fashioned iron key led them inside with a resounding click. Through the window, Rosalie saw a dining room and stairs leading up to the second floor. The realtor pushed open the grand door and led them into the house.

There was a smell of fresh country air coming in from the dining room windows. A huge family room to the right looked out onto the front of the house. The kitchen was to the left and had a large window that overlooked the side entrance steps. From the window you could see the circular driveway and the never ending mountains across the road. The bathroom off the dining room, back porch, and den off the kitchen made up the downstairs.

The stairs leading upstairs were beautiful. Mom, Dad, Rosalie, and Michael walked behind the realtor up six steps. Rosalie and Michael stopped at a landing with a window box that had a small handle. It looked out over the garden. The staircase then turned and there were another six steps that led upstairs. There was a large piece of wood, painted white that resembled the plank of a pirate ship that hugged the stairs opposite the wall.

Once upstairs there was a big door to the right. It opened into the biggest bathroom Rosalie had ever seen. It was the size of her bedroom back home. The windows overlooked the backyard and had little handles similar to the one on the window box. Surrounding the sink mirror were colorful hand painted pansies in hues of purples and blues. They left the bathroom and saw three bedrooms. The one immediately down the hall from the bathroom had two twin beds on either side of a window and Rosalie knew this was for her and Michael. It overlooked the front of the house. Looking outside she saw the slate porch. She imagined waking up and looking at the corn fields or seeing cows across the road. Those majestic mountains would be her view and to the right she could see the garage by the side of the road. The room had a window high above the dresser that was one of the smiling eyebrow windows. Mom and Dad's room was next to theirs. They had the same view and they also had a window that looked like the smiling eyebrow. The third bedroom was across from her parents' and Rosalie saw that it overlooked the backyard. There was a red metal circular garden and then a grassy hill that had an apple tree, perfect for climbing.

In the distance was the Unadilla River which flowed slowly around the bend. The rushing sound of water could be heard in the distance. Papers were drawn up, hands shook, and the family headed back to Brooklyn. They had a summer house and would be coming back in a few weeks.

SUMMER OF 1972

Dad and Mom packed up their clothes in plastic bags. Dad said they could fit more in the trunk of their car if they used large garbage bags instead of luggage. While Dad packed the car, Mom was in the kitchen with Rosalie and Michael. Mom emptied out all the sliced bread from the plastic sleeve in which it came onto a string of paper towels. She put the slices of bread into two neat rows and proceeded to cover one row with peanut butter and the other row with grape jelly. Michael and Rosalie worked like an assembly line marrying the two rows of bread into sandwiches and placing them in individual plastic bags. Then Mom put them all back into the plastic sleeve as if the loaf of bread had never been touched.

They wouldn't be coming back to Brooklyn until Labor Day. Rosalie went upstairs to her room one final time and used her finger to etch a cross in the carpeting in her closet. It was her way of saying goodbye to her room; hoping all of her toys and dolls would be safe while they were gone. She took Ted, her bear and lifelong friend and hopped into the back seat of the car with Michael. They rolled out of their driveway and were on the road. It was June. Driving to South New Berlin, Rosalie kept Ted on her lap and held him up to the window so he could see where they were going. A half hour into the drive Dad asked for a sandwich and some pretzels. With the hum of the road beneath her feet, Rosalie dozed off. Ted feel asleep too.

She woke up as they were driving down Route 8, minutes away from South New Berlin. On the left hand side of the road they passed a sign that read, "Welcome to South New Berlin". Then they came to a light, their light.

The town was small with one intersection at the cross section of Route 8 and Route 23. At the four corners there was a gas station on the left and across from that was Toby's Antiques. A man was sitting on an old rocking chair, rocking back and forth. Rosalie assumed he was Toby. To the right was an old house with a big porch and across the street was Madison's grocery store. Down the road past Madison's was a library.

They turned right onto Route 23, crossed over the Unadilla River, and made a left at a big yellow house. There were horses grazing in the field.

They passed a red barn and a white house with green shutters. The house was close to the road and the mailbox said Jensson. The Barr-Y Motel and swimming hole was on the right. The road was slow and their car left a gust of dirt and smoke behind it. You could hear pebbles kicking up from beneath their car.

Further down they drove through a bee swarm where white boxes lined the left side of the road. Another red barn with large doors was around the bend, signaling they were nearly home. Rosalie lifted Ted so he could be the first to see their house. The car slowed as they approached the green garage. Dad turned on the signal to make a left into the circular driveway and came to a stop in front of their house with the smiling eyebrows.

UNPACKING

Mom, Rosalie, and Michael helped Dad unpack. There was a slight breeze and not a cloud in the sky on this perfect June day. The family worked liked ants carrying bags into the house, heading back to the car for the next load. Back and forth, back and forth. In the distance, Rosalie saw two children riding bikes their way. It was a boy and girl, a little bit older than Rosalie, but not much. They pulled in and came to a stop straggling their legs on either side of their bikes.

"Hey there," said the girl.

Everyone stopped what they were doing. Rosalie stayed by her parents. The boy and girl hopped off their bikes leaving them lifeless on the ground and walked over to them. Dad extended his arm to shake their hands and introduced himself.

"Bought the Aider's house?" the girl asked.

"We did. I'm Dominick and this is my wife, Lillian. This is Rosalie," and he pointed to her, "and this is Michael," signaling to her brother. Rosalie lifted her arm to wave and then buried her head into the side of Dad's body.

"Mrs. Aider's name was Rosie too. I'm Ana and this is my brother Finn. We own the farm down the road. Mem and Heit said you'd be coming today. We saw you pull in."

"Saw us pull in? It had to be almost a mile away," thought Rosalie. She realized they were going to have to buy binoculars. Ana said school had just gotten out. She pointed to the field across the road filled with cows. "Those are our brothers out there in the field; Thomas, Liam, John, and Luke. They're bringing the cows in so we can't stay long. We just wanted to say hello. Have to get back to help with feeding. Mem is making zucchini bread to bring over to you later tonight."

"Who are Mem and Heit?" asked Rosalie.

"That's what I call my mom and dad. We're from Holland," said Ana.

She was an assertive girl. Polite but confident. Her brother didn't say much other than an occasional, "Yep" and nod of his head. And just like that, they were back on their bikes and disappeared in the distance between the two homes. Other than a small house next to their farm, they were their neighbors. Over the next 45 years, Rosalie and Michael would walk that road thousands of times to and from the de Vrie farm.

As they left Ana said, "Good-bye Rosie. Do they call you Rosie?"

Rosalie laughed and said, "No, I'm Roe".

Mom looked at Dad with a smile and said, "I guess we're going to have company tonight. We should get back to unpacking."

At 7:30 p.m. a station wagon pulled in. The de Vries poured out of their car slowly. The children followed their parents to the side porch entry like tired ducklings. They opened the screen door and piled into the porch. The large wooden door leading into the side entry of the house had a bell. Not a door bell, an actual bell. It hung on the right hand side of their wooden door. It was a black cast bell with a clapper that created a melodic ping. Mr. de Vrie gave the clapper a flick with his finger. "Ping!"

The de Vries were tall. All of them. They had a Dutch accent and Rosalie had a hard time understanding what they were saying at first. Mrs. de Vrie introduced herself first. Her name was Theresa. She had a face filled with character and a big smile. She wore no makeup, had beautiful hair, and was a sturdy woman. She was extremely smart, spoke with confidence, and had a warmth about her. Mr. de Vrie was a tall lanky man with kind eyes. His name was Finnegan. He was handsome and looked like something out of a Norman Rockwell painting. Standing in a row were their six children.

Thomas was the oldest. He wore glasses, was gentle, slender, and looked more like a scientist than a farmer. Next was Liam. He stood out from the others with his movie star looks and smile. He was taller than Thomas and more outgoing, charismatic, with a birthmark on the side of his nose that added even more character to his face. He didn't look like a farmer either. John was tall and thin. He was handsome, shy, and quiet. Luke was all boy, smiling with a sense of mischief. Ana had long blonde hair and was eager to have a girl in her life now. Looking at her the entire time, Rosalie knew she and Ana would become friends. Finn was the youngest, fidgeting, transferring his weight from one foot to the next.

Everyone shook hands which took a long time. There were a lot of smiles and nice to meet yous. Mrs. de Vrie had the promised zucchini bread in her hands and they all settled around the dining room table for a quick visit. Rosalie had never had zucchini bread and was not really interested in a dessert made of a vegetable. It was green and bits of zucchini were growing out of the sides of the bread. Mom made the best chocolate chip cookies and Rosalie was thinking how great they would be right now. She realized Mrs. de Vrie wasn't the type of person you said no to. She sat there looking at the slice of zucchini bread on her place, poking at it with her fork. She put the smallest piece in her mouth. Shocked, she found herself enjoying it. Rosalie looked up, took the moment in, watching everyone eating, smiling, parents laughing and talking, and she knew life was good. They had neighbors, good neighbors.

HORSEBACK RIDING

Mom grew up in Manhattan, New York; however, she grew up loving Roy Rogers, King of the Cowboys. She would watch him and his horse Trigger on TV. He was her childhood hero and because she talked about him so much, Rosalie grew up thinking somehow he was a distant relative of hers. Grandma Rose would laugh and tell Rosalie, "I love your mom, but I think the stork brought her to the wrong house. It should have dropped her off somewhere in the country."

Mom was in her element in New York State. She loved the wide open spaces and seeing wildlife right outside the house. Most of all, Mom loved horses.

They drove to the Barr-Y for their first horseback riding lesson. What she thought when she got out of the car was that horses smell, but it was a smell she loved immediately. Dad loved it too.

It was warm outside, but not too hot and the horses were in the barn. A woman with a cowboy hat was putting a saddle on one horse. It was a western saddle with a horn that Rosalie figured would come in handy if she started to fall off. She climbed on and looked down at her parents who were smiling at her with pride. The woman led Rosalie to a field that was surrounded with high grass. Mom, Dad, and Michael watched from a distance. Sitting on the horse and moving to the rhythm of his gate could have lulled her to sleep. Rosalie was hooked. After 15 minutes her ride was up and the woman led the horse with Rosalie on top back to the long grass and her family. She got off, Michael got on. He was two years younger than her. Rosalie loved her brother. He smiled a lot and everyone said he was adorable. As they watched Michael on the horse walking away, Mom and Dad started talking with Rosalie about her ride. They asked her what it felt like and if she enjoyed it. The conversation lasted only a few minutes, because when Dad looked up he exclaimed, "Oh no! Michael's not on the horse."

There past the long grass was a horse with no rider. Just a horse. Dad started running and Mom and Rosalie stayed back. "He's okay," said the woman.

Next thing Rosalie saw was Michael in Dad's arms. He dusted him off and put him right back on the horse. "Hold onto the horn," Rosalie yelled, pointing to the top of the saddle.

Michael smiled from the saddle and yelled back, both hands on the horn, "It happened so fast."

The ride ended. Mom and Dad signed Rosalie and Michael up for weekly riding lessons. Then everyone got back into the car. They smelled like horses and before long, their car smelled of horses too. Dad rolled the window down and waved his hand in front of his nose smiling.

They headed to Madison's Grocery Store in town for ice cream. The old man, who Mrs. de Vrie confirmed was in fact Toby, was sitting in the rocking chair outside of Toby's Antiques. He just rocked back and forth, watching the cars drive by.

There was furniture in the front of his store, set up like the inside of a house.

As they headed home, Mom insisted Rosalie and Michael take their pants off on the front porch and head straight into the bathtub. They did and ran upstairs. Rosalie ran the tub and Michael filled it with bubble bath. Rosalie jumped into the warm water when Mom came in. Leaning over the tub Mom laughed thinking about the day, washing dirt off of her hands, and gently shampooing her hair.

Out of the tub, she dried off in her room and got dressed. Mom ran the tub again for Michael, who put in extra bubble bath. Once the smell of horse was washed away, Mom wrapped Michael in a towel, and dried his hair. Then everyone headed downstairs in their pajamas. The smell of the horses came back when Mom walked by with their dirty clothes. Everything went into the washing machine and they sat down for Mom's amazing chicken cutlets for dinner.

The buzzer of the washing machine went off and Mom headed outside with the clean wet clothes. She hung them on the clothes line to dry. It wasn't a regular clothes line like Grandma had. It looked like a beach umbrella without the umbrella. Lines were strung in squares that grew smaller and smaller from the perimeter of the clothes line to the pole in the center that held it into the ground. When Mom brought the clothes in after they were dry, they were the best smelling clothes Rosalie had ever had. They smelled of the country air.

AAGE JENSSON

An old man was riding a lawnmower down the road. Rosalie didn't know what he was mowing, but he just kept getting closer and closer to their house, moving at a really slow rate. Then she saw him pull into their circular driveway. "There's a man riding a lawnmower outside," Rosalie said to Mom.

"I've got it," Dad said getting up from the pile of paperwork at the dining room table. He went outside and Michael and Rosalie ran to the window putting their hands on the sill.

The man was wrinkled with smiling eyes. He was tall and thin wearing olive green pants, a flannel shirt, and work boots. It was summer and Rosalie thought he must have been pretty hot wearing all those clothes. He shook Dad's hands and introduced himself.

"I'm Aage Jensson. Live down the road by the Pemberton house at the corner. I've got the big red barn and my house is next to it. Built it myself. The de Vries told me you bought the Aider's house and said you came from the city. Figured you'd need someone to mow the lawn."

His voice was slow and rolled off his lips like a lazy river.

Rosalie was shocked. "He drove all the way from the end of the road? It had to be more than two miles…on a lawnmower!"

Dad led Aage into the house. He said hello to Mom, ruffled Michael's hair, and gave Rosalie a cheerful "How do you do?"

He didn't have all his fingers and Michael and Rosalie couldn't stop staring at his hand. He noticed and they felt bad.

"Lost them over the years," said Aage and then he ruffled Michael's hair again.

He was a funny old man with no teeth. When he smiled his whole face lifted up as if there were strings attached to the sides of his mouth. Rosalie liked him. She liked him a lot.

He and Dad went back outside and shook hands. Aage would be mowing the lawn and Rosalie was excited because that meant he'd be by every week.

PAINTING ROCKS

On Sunday night Dad had to head back to Brooklyn for work. Mom, Rosalie, and Michael walked to the mailbox. Dad pulled out of the driveway by the de Vrie side of their home. As he slowly drove by he would roll down the window and say, "With God all things are possible". That is what Dad always said. They would wave back and watch him disappear around the bend.

Right by the mailbox was their waving place. They would stay upstate with Mom until Dad returned on Friday. He would be bringing Grandma Rose and Grandma Rosalie.

That night lightly sleeping in their beds, they waited for the phone to ring twice signaling that Dad had safely arrived home. Outside, the only sounds were of crickets and the trees blowing in the gentle wind.

"With God all things are possible," thought Rosalie and she drifted off to sleep.

Mom got them up early. They got dressed, had breakfast, and headed out the door. Mom had a red wagon lined with pillows from the couch waiting for them outside. She put Michael and Rosalie in it and started walking down the road, pulling them along. They stopped at the de Vrie field that had just been mowed. There were straight lines in the dirt and rocks were sitting on the top of the ground like large potatoes, the size of basketballs. They got out of the wagon and Mom handed Rosalie and Michael their pillows. She started putting the large stones in the little red wagon.

"What are you doing with the stones?" Rosalie asked.

"We're going to paint them and line our driveway with them! I called Mrs. de Vrie and she said we'd be doing her a favor."

Mom loaded up the wagon, headed home, unloaded the wagon, put Rosalie and Michael back in, headed back to the field, unloaded the children, loaded up the wagon with rocks, back and forth they went, six times. When Mom wanted to do something, she did it. Despite the fact that Mom is a very thin, petite woman, she had the strength of an ox.

When they were done, they had a pile of thirty rocks by the water pump that looked like a pumpkin patch. Mom pulled the handle up, then pushed it down, pulled it up again, then pushed down, up and down. Water started coming out! She started washing those rocks, scrubbing them with her hands. Rosalie and Michael helped as Mom continued pumping the water. The water was cold and felt nice on the warm day as it splattered up from the rocks onto their faces. The rocks were sparkling clean and the sun dried them in no time.

After lunch they headed into town with their little red wagon and pillows that made the ride more comfortable. Around the bend, Mom stopped. There was a wall of bees in the middle of the road. Rosalie and Michael had never seen anything like it before.

A woman came out from the house on the other side of the road. She was a lively woman with a giggle in her voice.

"Hey there! Don't mind the bees. If you walk through the swarm slowly they won't bother you."

They didn't believe her and she sensed their hesitation.

She shouted again with her giggling voice, "I'm Mrs. Bibble. Those are MY bees. We make honey. When you get through I'll give you a jar to take home!"

All of a sudden, Mom started toward the bees. Rosalie and Michael looked at each other in absolute disbelief. Mom turned and looked at Rosalie and Michael sternly. "Not a move," and they didn't. Rosalie pressed her lips together and thought about closing her eyes and then decided against it. Her lips stayed together fiercely, to the point where it was almost uncomfortable, but those lips weren't moving.

What seemed like forever, they slowly walked through the bees. Rosalie didn't move her head but gave her peripheral vision a run for its money. Bees were flying all around them but never came near the little red wagon. Rosalie looked at Michael whose eyes were wide and full of shock. Buzzing was all around them and the hum was almost calming, but not enough to relieve their fear. As the bees were buzzing behind them, they emerged from the swarm. Mrs. Bibble approached them with open arms.

"Look at these beautiful children! You must be the folks that bought the Aider's house. I was talking with Theresa de Vrie and she told us you had moved in. Summer folk here from down state."

Everyone seemed to know the Aiders and apparently the de Vries.

Mrs. Bibble and Mom talked for a bit and then she disappeared into her house. She returned with a jar of honey. Mom put it in the wagon in between Rosalie and Michael and they continued their journey down the road. Mrs. Bibble waved good-bye until they couldn't see her anymore.

They passed Aage Jensson's house. He was outside his barn with a saw in his hand. He smiled and waved as they passed. Mom let him know they were heading into town and would stop by on the way back. Madison's was just a little way down Route 23, just past the bridge. The Unadilla River was much louder here, raging beneath them.

Outside of Madison's they left the wagon and headed in. Toby was in his rocking chair where they left him from their last visit into town. There was a bell on the inside of the door that rang when they opened it. This was the smallest grocery store Rosalie had ever seen. There was only one register, but everything they needed was there, including ice cream. Michael and Rosalie ran to the freezer and reached in for fudgsicles, but Mom stopped them in their tracks.

"After I get the paint, okay?"

It seemed like a fair deal so they headed to the back of the store and picked up some white paint. Mom paid the cashier and told them to get their ice cream, and get one for her too.

They sat outside eating ice cream, and Mom put the cans of paint in the little red wagon. It was getting a little tight in there with the paint and honey, but it was a beautiful day and they walked home enjoying the sights. Other than Toby, things looked different in the wagon. You miss a lot driving by in a car.

Aage was still outside hammering nails into wood. He looped the hammer into his belt loop and walked toward the road, wiping his brow with a piece of cloth he removed from his back pocket. He looked down at Rosalie and Michael in the little red wagon and then noticed the paint.

"Doin' some painting?"

Mom lit up and told him about the rocks. Aage didn't look as excited about the idea as Mom. He put his hand over his mouth and stroked his chin over and over again like he was thinking hard. Then he just said, "Okay then," as if the idea left him.

Mom let him know they had met Mrs. Bibble and about the bees and the honey, and then Aage wiped his forehead again and said he had to get back to work. Aage walked as slowly as he talked.

Rosalie and Michael were excited to pass the Barr-Y and see the horses outside. The wind blew the air with their scent and Rosalie smiled thinking about her riding lesson next week. Throughout their walk she and Michael got in and out of the wagon, which made pulling the wagon easier for Mom.

As they got closer to home Rosalie started thinking about those bees again, and hopped back in the wagon with Michael, but she wasn't as concerned. If they left the bees alone, the bees would leave them alone. Mom managed the little red wagon through the swarm again, Rosalie's lips pressed together, but not as hard this time. She was actually able to breathe normally and her mouth didn't hurt.

There would be no painting today. Instead they made dinner and watched TV. Michael and Rosalie didn't ever argue about what show to watch. There was only one channel on their TV because of the reception in the country. Whatever was on channel 4 was what they watched.

Mom pulled out a puzzle and dumped out all the pieces onto the card table in the family room. Mom is a master puzzle maker. She let Michael and Rosalie sort out all the edges and then put all the middle pieces back into the box. While it was time consuming sorting all those pieces, it was also very relaxing. It was getting close to their bedtime so it was time for baths, a story, and prayers.

They all knelt by the side of Michael's bed; which was to the left side of the window. There was a picture of a boy over his bed and a picture of a girl standing on a swing above Rosalie's. Rosalie loved that she shared her wall with Mom and Dad.

"God is good. God is great.
Let us thank Him for this beautiful day.

Now I lay me down to sleep.
I pray the Lord my soul to keep.
If I should die before I wake,
I pray the Lord my soul to take.
If I should live for other days,
I pray the Lord to guide my ways.

God Bless Mommy and Daddy, Rosalie and Michael, our Aunts and Uncles, our Grandmas and Grandpas, cousins, and friends.

With God all things are possible."

Every night that is what they said all kneeling by the bed. Mom tucked them in and turned off the lights. From the window they heard an owl. The fresh air came in from the window. With Ted next to her, his head on the pillow, Rosalie kept her hand on the wall until she fell asleep with the comfort of knowing Mom was right next door.

That week they painted rocks. They painted the tops of the rocks, the sides of the rocks, and the bottom of the rocks. Mom laid a sheet out so that they didn't get the lawn covered in paint. They put two coats on the rocks and waited for them to dry.

One by one, Mom lined the inside and outside of the driveway with the big beautiful white rocks. Dad would be home soon and she wanted it done for his arrival. The white rocks stood out on the green grass and created a welcoming pathway for Dad. From around the bend they saw his car. Mom rushed to the front of the house waving as he pulled in. They saw his smile and amazement when he noticed all the rocks.

The grandmas were with him and they were waving from the car as it came to a stop. Dad opened the door and bounded out picking Mom up in his arms giving her a kiss.

"This looks FANTATIC!" he said and kissed her again.

"I love my parents," thought Rosalie with a smile.

Dad knelt down and gave Rosalie and Michael a big group hug. The car doors swung open and out came the grandmas, with hugs, kisses, and gum. They would be spending the summer with them upstate, this year and every year.

Grandma Rose was Mom's mom and Grandma Rosalie was Dad's mom. They became best friends when Mom and Dad got married. Two very different women with two very different stories, both filled with lots of love for their children and grandchildren.

Grandma Rose was tall and thin. She had naturally dark hair even though she was a grandma. Grandma Rose always brought Rosalie and Michael gum in a brown paper lunch bag hidden in her big black purse. And Grandma Rose made great meatballs. Although quiet, Grandma Rose was always smiling and never thought grandchildren should get reprimanded. "They're good," is what she always said.

Grandma Rosalie taught Grandma Rose how to crochet. They both wore dresses most of the time. Grandma Rose was very loving so when anyone was down or need a hug, she let you know everything was going to be okay. She didn't worry about the small stuff in life and her family was everything to her.

Grandma Rosalie was short. She had grey hair and was the smartest woman Rosalie knew. She was a business woman and was great with money. Every day she sat at the kitchen table and did the crossword puzzle. Grandpa Andrea died two years ago, so she enjoyed spending time with Grandma Rose. Grandma Rosalie and Grandpa Andrea really loved each other and Rosalie knew she missed him a lot.

Rosalie was named after Grandma Rosalie and Michael was named after Dad's older brother, Uncle Mike. Uncle Mike was the funniest man she knew and always called them with a joke. Rosalie knew he would want to visit them because he loved the country.

Grandma Rosalie carried her crocheting bag with her everywhere and whenever she had a minute, it came out. When she laughed, Rosalie laughed with her because her love of life was infectious. However, she was a very strong woman and when Rosalie needed to have a serious discussion, Grandma Rosalie was the person she talked with because she was so wise. Grandma Rosalie prayed for everyone each morning and night. And Grandma Rosalie always had Licorice Chips and Chicklets in her purse. When they visited her in Brooklyn, she always made sure there were Italian cookies in her cookie tin.

Rosalie loved her grandmas. They were both very soft and when Rosalie was tired, she liked to fall asleep on their laps.

MAKING A HOUSE A HOME

Since Dad was going to be taking their car back every Sunday, they needed things to do around the house to keep busy. There was a rhubarb patch by the driveway. Rosalie and Michael had never seen plants so big. Rhubarb looked like huge pink celery with fans as leaves. Grandma Rosalie said it was good for pie. Inspired, Mom decided she wanted to put in a garden, but not a little one, an enormous one.

The de Vries came over and helped them till the soil. Mrs. de Vrie was a master gardener and grew vegetables to last her family throughout the winter. They planted pole beans, carrots, zucchini, cucumbers, onions, corn, tomatoes, peppers, lettuce, parsley, basil, pumpkins, and watermelon. Aage said he would help with the potatoes. It was a long day, but they planted and planted row after row of seeds, and then they watered and watered and watered some more. They left a big section for Aage's potatoes.

The next day coming down the road was Aage on his lawnmower. He was pulling a wagon behind the mower and it was filled with potatoes and shovels. When he got to their house, he look around and scratched his head. He had to mow the lawn.

He started at the beginning of the circular driveway and proceeded to pick up every big white rock and move it from the grass to the graveled driveway. One by one he moved the rocks and then turned to the other side and moved all those rocks off the lawn to the inside of the graveled driveway.

Dad looked outside and told Mom, "The next time Aage comes we should move the rocks for him. And I'll let him know we'll move the rocks back today so he doesn't have to do it." Dad was always thinking about other people. They went outside and Aage came over.

"Your wife really likes these rocks. It looks mighty nice....," his words trailed off.

Dad stopped him. "Sorry about that. We'll make sure the rocks are moved before you get here the next time, and the kids will put them back onto the lawn when you're done with the lawn. Why don't you come in for a cup of coffee?"

"Don't mind if I do," said Aage as he walked behind Dad into the house.

Michael and Rosalie looked at each other. Those rocks were big.

After coffee, Aage finished up the lawn and then headed over to the garden to meet Dad. He wiped his brow with the cloth from his olive green work pants and gave Mom an approving nod. It was an impressive view. Neat rows of dirt all labeled with different vegetables and spices.

Aage brought the wagon over that was attached to his lawn mower. It was filled with cut up potatoes. He had a whole one in his hands, took out a pocket knife, and explained that you needed to cut the potato up into pieces, but it had to have eyes on it. Rosalie had no idea what he was talking about and he saw the perplexed look on her face.

Leaning down to Rosalie and Michael Aage said, "You see here, all these parts here? They're potato eyes. You gotta have two eyes to plant the potato. You see?"

They nodded and Aage continued, "And the potato has to heal after you cut it, so I cut these up yesterday for your folks. So, now we have to dig some holes, okay?"

Aage's eyes always looked like he was trying to keep the sun out of them, even when it wasn't sunny. He had light blue eyes that sparkled and the way he spoke reminded Rosalie of a slow song floating down a lazy river. He was a bit of a character, and although he looked a little rocky, was very healthy and strong.

Aage picked up a shovel from the back of the wagon and started digging. Grandma Rose and Grandma Rosalie came out from the back porch with a load of wet clothes and started hanging laundry on the clothes line. Aage dug a hole about six inches deep and then took three steps in a straight line and dug another hole. Three more steps, another hole.

He turned around and told Dad to get the bucket out of the wagon. Michael put his nose to the bucket and came up quick. "That does not smell good," he said, wrinkling his nose.

Aage told Dad to follow him, putting a little shovel of whatever was in his bucket into the hole. They worked together row after row. When they were done Aage started down the row again and put a piece of potato onto the smelly rotten dirt, cut side down. Dad followed him with the bucket of dirt, putting it on top of the seed potato.

Mom, Michael, and Rosalie decided to roll the big white rocks back onto the lawn.

When they got back to the garden, Grandma Rose and Grandma Rosalie were sitting outside in chairs. It was hot and Michael started playing in the dirt. He sat right down in it as if he were at the beach.

Mom took out the hose to water the garden while Michael got dirtier and dirtier. Eventually the dirt was mud and Michael just kept playing and playing. Soon he was covered in mud, smiling, and then just laid down in it. Everyone thought it was funny, especially Aage who walked over to Michael and ruffled his mud-matted hair.

"You got a good boy here Dominick, a good boy. Gonna have to clean him up with that hose though before you let him the house."

And with that, Michael stood up and stretched out his arms. Mom put the hose on the mist setting and cleaned him up. He turned around so she could get his back too.

Seeing that Michael was already wet, Mom decided to attach the sprinkler to the hose and let Rosalie and Michael play outside. They ran through the sprinkler on the wet grass while the grandmas crocheted and sipped water in the shade.

The weekend ended as it always did. Dad left to go back to Brooklyn every Sunday night. As they stood by the waving place, he rolled the window down and said, "With God all things are possible."

They would all wait for the phone to ring twice signaling his safe arrival. Dad would return every Thursday for a long weekend, but sometimes he had to work until Friday. Rosalie loved waiting by the mailbox, seeing Dad's car peering around the bend, and then yelling to Mom, "He's here!   He's here!" while Michael echoed, "He's here!" running behind her.

A CALF NAMED LILLIAN

They were now settled into their new home. From time to time, Mrs. de Vrie would come over with Ana and Finn for a visit. She would talk with Grandma Rosalie and Grandma Rose sharing crocheting patterns and taking about blankets and hats.

On this particular beautiful summer day, Mom had just finished making banana bread. She said they should bring it to the de Vries.

They headed down the road around 3:30 p.m., Rosalie and Michael nestled in the little red wagon. Mom hoped to get to the farm in time for tea. All the boys and Mr. de

Vrie came in from the fields for tea every day at 4:00. Then they would head into the barn to feed and milk the cows.

Cows smell different from horses, and not in a good way, at least in Rosalie's mind. The de Vrie farm was big and their house was big too. It was three stories high and the biggest house Rosalie had ever been in.

An enclosed porch ran the entire length of the front of the de Vrie house. Outside there were clothes drying on a clothes line, but their clothes line ran from the front of their house to the top of their garage. A bucket of clothespins was outside on the steps. Their dairy farm and silos were across the road.

Mom knocked on the screen door because there was no doorbell. Mrs. de Vrie came out, her hair was pinned up with a clip. She was excited to see Mom and ever more excited when she saw the banana bread.

Ana was setting the table and waved Rosalie over to join her. Ana said hello and handed her a tea cup. "Want to help me set the table?"

As Ana walked around the table putting down saucers, Rosalie followed putting teacups on top. They sat down around the large aqua-blue rectangular kitchen table. In the center of the table was a ceramic bowl with tiny teaspoons in it.

Then, one by one the de Vrie boys came in. The screen door opened, boots came off, the door slammed shut, and someone would walk in. They didn't say much, other than Liam, who had a story and a smile. He told Mom a cow was in labor and if they stayed after tea they could probably see a calf being born.

The banana bread was still warm. Mrs. de Vrie came to the table with two tall cookie tins. They had pictures of windmills on them and were filled to the top, bursting with homemade chocolate chip cookies.

Mr. de Vrie poured everyone tea. Rosalie had a piece of Mom's banana bread and Mrs. de Vrie offered Michael and Rosalie each a cookie, which they took. Michael said he was thirsty, but did not want tea, so Ana got up and got a bucket out of the refrigerator. A bucket! It was filled with milk.

Rosalie's eyes widened thinking, "Now, I'm not a big milk drinker, but I know that the milk at our house comes in a carton. We're at a dairy farm, so that milk just came out of a cow."

Being that she was already not a fan of milk, Rosalie wasn't trying it, but Michael did. She watched him as he took a sip, wondering if he was going to spit it out everywhere.

"It's good. It tastes like milk," and he finished his glass.

Yuck. Rosalie made a face and Mom gave her a look and shook her head. Rosalie looked at Ana who was laughing. She laughed back and knew now that they were friends.

Rosalie liked Ana. She was a free spirit, spoke her mind, and could beat up most boys Rosalie knew back home. Not that she would, but she could. Mom spoke with Mr. and Mrs. de Vrie while the boys drank their tea and ate their banana bread in silence. Liam picked Michael up and started playing with him, until Mr. de Vrie announced it was milking time. Liam still had Michael in his arms and said, "Do you want to see a calf being born?"

Michael look at him with wide eyes and said, "Yes!"

Liam threw Michael onto his shoulders and Mom followed them out the door. Rosalie stayed back with Ana cleaning up the dishes and then they raced over to the barn. What she walked into was nothing short of shocking.

The cow was breathing heavily and standing up, her stomach rapidly going in and out. There were feet coming out of her. Feet! Mr. de Vrie tied a rope to the legs, walked to the other side of the milking aisle and walked the rope around a pole that went from the floor to the ceiling.

"Sometimes they need a little help," he said still looking intently at the cow.

She looked back and gave a big MOO! Mom was holding Michael now and Rosalie was standing next to Mom with Ana. Little by little the feet became legs. Then the cow laid down and the legs became a head. Once the head was out, it was quick. In an instant, an entire calf was on the hay of the barn floor. John walked over and said it was a heifer calf.

Ana leaned over and said, "That means it is a girl, which is good because we'll keep her. She'll become a milker."

"What happens to the boys?"

"The boys are bull calves and they get taken to the auction, but sometimes we keep them."

Finn and Luke went to the cow and rubbed her head, while Thomas checked the calf. The cow reached back and started to clean the calf. It was the most amazing thing Rosalie had ever seen. Within no time, the calf was up and walking. Mom was in Heaven. She thanked Mr. de Vrie over and over again for allowing them to see this beautiful event. She knew they had a lot of work to do and the calf delayed milking for them.

Before they left, John came over with a kitten. Softly he said that one of their cats just had a litter and wanted to know if they wanted to see them. In the back of the barn, nestled between two bales of hay were three little kittens. John put the fourth one back with the others. He was kind and had a gentle heart. He knelt down and gently patted each kitten.

Mom said they had to get home, so they said their goodbyes and Ana walked them back to the house on the other side of the road. Rosalie asked Ana if the cows had names and was surprised when she said yes. Ana said their cows are pets to them and they not only have names, but they *know* all their cows.

There were 200 cows in that barn and Rosalie was happy they all had names. It made each one of them special. Ana said they would probably name cows after everyone in Rosalie's family.

The one that was born that day was named Lillian, after Mom. And there would be a Rosalie before summer's end.

Dad returned that night and Mom told him all about the calf. He and Mom came upstairs and read Rosalie and Michael a story together. That night they said their prayers and then said a special one for the new calf, Lillian. With Ted by her side and her hand on the wall, Rosalie drifted off to sleep.

SIGRID AND A SURPRISE

While Aage was a man with a face filled with character, a heart full of love, a passion for life, and not a care in the world, he also had a wife. Rosalie could not have imagined two more different people. Aage's car pulled into their driveway. He came out of the car standing tall, looked up at the sun, and smiled. He was constantly smiling. He adjusted his glasses and looked up at the sky again. His pants were always a little too big for him, and his shirts hung on him loosely. He was not a messy man. In fact, other than his clothes being a little too big, he always looked quite nice.

Michael and Rosalie were by the window, noses pressed against the glass, hands on the window sill, and then they saw her. Sigrid Jensson.

Sigrid looked like something out of magazine. Her hair was perfectly done and she was impeccably dressed with fancy pants, a ruffled shirt, and a matching purse. Not what they expected. She had a stern look about her and walked with a mission. This woman was all business. Michael and Rosalie looked at each other and decided to get busy with a puzzle, any puzzle.

Aage and Sigrid entered the house as if announced at a ball. Sigrid stood in the doorway, purse over her forearm, and put her hand out to Mom.

With a firm handshake she gave Mom a curt and straightforward, "Hello. I am Sigrid Jensson."

She looked about the house with a keen eye taking inventory of their belongings, including Rosalie and Michael. Mom called the children over and they stood up as straight as they could, shoulders back. Sigrid looked at them and gave a quick smile and a "How do you do?" Rosalie felt like she should curtsy, but didn't.

"I'm Mrs. Jensson," she said sternly, "and I make very good molasses cookies." Then she smiled.

Rosalie and Michael looked at each other not sure what to make of Sigrid. She turned and sat down in a dining room chair. Her purse was on her lap. At the dining room table, Mrs. Jensson quickly gave Mom the inside scoop of South New Berlin and caught her up on all the town gossip. Mom just listened, occasionally replying with a "Wow" or a "Hmmm".

Aage asked for something stronger than coffee to drink. Mom and Dad didn't drink anything stronger than coffee, but Dad had what Aage wanted in the liquor cabinet. He poured him a small drink and while the women visited, Aage and Dad headed outside to talk about something privately. Dad told Rosalie and Michael to stay inside as it was a surprise. Rosalie loved surprises, but liked them better when she knew what they were or was involved in planning the surprise.

After an hour, Dad and Aage were in Aage's car heading down the road to the de Vries' farm. They were gone for a while and returned with a tire. Rosalie thought Aage had a flat, but instead of fixing the flat, Aage started rolling the tire around to the back of the house.

Dad headed to the tool shed nestled in the back left hand corner of the property. A big tree behind the shed hung over it. Its branches looked as though they were trying to protect the shed from the sun. Dad disappeared in there for a while. He came out with a long rope.

Michael and Rosalie ran out the back porch and asked Dad what he and Aage were doing. "Come on." he said. "We're putting up a tire swing for the two of you."

Michael and Rosalie jumped up and down screaming with delight, hugging each other in between leaps and shrills.

Aage was by the butternut tree in the back yard looking up and scratching his head. Dad walked over and they began strategizing how to hang the tire. With the rope knotted at one end, Dad tossed the rope up and over the large branch extending out

20 feet above him. Aage looped the rope through the tire, pulled it to lift the tire off the ground, and secured a knot.

"Who wants to try this out first?"

"Let's go on together," Michael said. Dad put Michael in the tire facing one way and Rosalie on top facing Michael. Mom, Sigrid, and the grandmas came out to see the first push. The tire swung back and forth and then started spinning slowly around as they flew through the air. Lemonade was brought out and the adults talked with each other, laughing occasionally. Sigrid's pinky could be seen when she took a sip of lemonade. Rosalie thought she would try to hold her pinky out when she had some lemonade later.

Rosalie and Michael were still on the swing when Aage and Sigrid left. As they pulled away, Aage stuck his arm out the window and waved. He gave a toot of his horn. Sigrid looked straight ahead, purse on lap.

Dad left on Sunday. Grandma Rose and Grandma Rosalie came to the waving place with Mom, Rosalie, and Michael as they sent Dad on his drive back to Brooklyn. "With God all things are possible."

They watch him disappear around the bend. Holding hands, they all walked back to the house with the smiling eyes. That night the grandmas sat on the couch crocheting while Mom stood over the game table with the children working on the puzzle until bedtime. That night they went up the crooked stairs, said prayers and Rosalie fell asleep, Ted next to her on her pillow, her hand on the wall. In the quiet of the night, the phone rang twice. Dad was safely home.

"With God all things are possible," thought Rosalie and she drifted off to sleep.

FISHING AND PARSLEY

The days of summer went by slowly and seemed like they would never end. That's how summer felt. It was forever. It was a warm day and Grandma Rose and Grandma Rosalie were in the kitchen making meatballs, doing laundry, and keeping themselves busy with daily chores of sweeping floors and doing dishes. Mom went outside and into the tool shed. She returned with two yellow plastic fishing poles and told Rosalie and Michael they were going to the Barr-Y.

They bounded upstairs, put on bathing suits, tossed on some shorts and t-shirts, and headed outside, pillows in hand. They got into the little red wagon holding their fishing poles, sitting comfortably on their pillows instead of the hard wood. At the end of the fishing line were two bobbins that looked like ping pong balls with a red stripe around each center. They arrived at the Barr-Y and walked to the dock in the center of the pond.

It was sunny outside and the sun's heat warmed their faces. Rosalie, Michael, and Mom sat down, feet over the side of the dock. Rosalie and Michael cast their lines, hoping to catch something.

Nothing.

Again and again they would reel their lines in, cast out, and patiently watch the bobbin floating on the surface of the murky pond rise and fall with the ripples of the water.

Nothing.

Sitting on the dock, Mom would tell stories about her childhood, growing up in Manhattan, her favorite teacher, winning the spelling bee, and her love of Roy Rogers.

They would sing the song she wrote, scaring away any fish that were remotely interested in their lines and plastic hooks.

Mom would start singing and then Rosalie and Michael would join her. This is Mom's song…

I love the wide open spaces, the way they used to be.

I remember when the animals were beautiful and free.

I remember how the birds would sing their little song,

And people wouldn't think of doin' wrong.

Why did they have to change it so? I loved the way it looked.

The only way I remember the West is by my history book.

Whenever I go fishing, I sing this little song.

It's all about the Great Big West and what we're doin' wrong.

With no luck of fish, they decided to get candy from the Snack Bar by the pool and head home.

As Mom pulled them in the wagon, Michael and Rosalie sang her song holding onto their fishing poles. They didn't know you had to put bait on the end of the pole; however, Mom did.

It wasn't about fishing. It was about sitting on that dock talking with each other, spending time together, and creating memories.

Grandma Rosalie and Grandma Rose were in the garden when they arrived home. They had made sauce while everyone was out and were now pulling weeds. They each had a bucket next to them and were both bent over diligently clearing the ground around the now green garden. Rosalie and Michael ran up to them, gave them hugs, and Grandma Rosalie asked if they caught dinner.

"Nope. But Mom let us go to the Snack Bar. We brought home chocolate bars."

Michael proudly showed them two chocolate bars, one in each hand. "Do you and Grandma want one?" he asked.

She smiled and said, "You and Rosalie can have them."

The garden was growing. Sprouting up from the ground were green signs of life. Rosalie thought to herself, "Imagine a family from Brooklyn, "city folk" they called us, growing a massive garden like this. We are country folk now."

Grandma Rosalie told Mom the parsley was up and was excited to use it in the sauce. Ever so carefully they all picked the parsley and brought it inside. This would be great for dinner tonight. Their own parsley on top of Grandma's sauce and meatballs. Mom had a table on the back porch and she lined it with a dish cloth. Everyone brought in handfuls of fresh parsley and Mom gingerly placed it in neat rows on the towel. It was beautiful.

They were all covered in dirt. It was on their hands, up their arms, and underneath their fingernails. Michael and Rosalie washed up in the downstairs bathroom, rubbing their hands together under the warm soapy water. Mom handed them an old toothbrush to get the dirt out from under their nails. Drying their hands, there was a knock on the door. It was Mrs. de Vrie and Ana coming for a visit. Mom let them in and proudly brought them to the back porch to show them the parsley drying on the back porch. Rosalie and Michael followed.

"Look what we have!"

Ana looked at the rows and rows of green leaves on the table, perplexed.

"Why did you cut off the tops of all the *carrots*?"

Mrs. de Vrie laughed. Mom started laughing too and then they all started laughing. They had some things to learn about gardening and living in the country.

PLANTING TREES

Dad came home late Thursday night, exhausted from the ride. It was raining which made the drive along the dark country roads that much slower. When Rosalie and Michael came downstairs the next morning, Dad was having coffee in his big white ceramic bowl. A box of cereal was on the kitchen table. Most people put milk on their cereal. Not Dad. He would put his cereal in his coffee. He said it was delicious.

Next to his bowl was a small glass for orange juice and on his napkin were two vitamins. Dad was so silly. He saw Rosalie and Michael coming into the kitchen and got up to get the orange juice out of the refrigerator. He held the juice while his whole body started to shake in uncontrollable spasms. Rosalie and Michael laughed and put their arms around Dad to stop him from shaking. As they held him tight, his body would stop shaking and the juice in his hands would start to shake. If they let him go, he would make his body shake again.

Sitting down, he poured the juice and put a vitamin barely into his mouth, lips pressed together around it. The vitamin hung from his mouth. Michael put his tiny fingers up against the vitamin and pushed it in. Dad took a sip of juice to wash it down. He put the second vitamin into his pursed lips and as if on que, Rosalie pushed it into his mouth. He took another sip of juice and the vitamin was gone.

Dad looked at the two of them. "So I thought we'd climb up the de Vrie mountain and dig up some trees to line the side of our property. Who wants to come with me? You can pick out your own trees."

Rosalie and Michael were so excited. They each had a bowl of cereal while Dad got the car ready. Then they jumped in the car and drove down their country road and up Route 23.

They had never made a left out of the road past Aage's house and wondered where it would take them. The road winded up the mountain and brought them to a clearing. Outside the view was majestic. The clearing overlooked Route 8. They saw the de Vrie's barn, the corn field, and their house. It looked so small.

They walked down the mountain a little ways and found saplings of evergreens that were strong and full of life. Michael pointed to two small trees growing next to each other and said he wanted them. Rosalie and Mom walked together holding hands and talking about their summer.

Mom was so beautiful. Her dark brown hair blew in the wind and the sun made her green eyes look like gems. Rosalie had green eyes too, just like Mom, but her hair was lighter. Mom knelt down by a sapling and Rosalie touched her Mom's hair.

Mom turned and looked lovingly at Rosalie, cradled her face in her hands and said, "When I was your age, I had light hair just like you and Michael. And as I got older it got darker and darker. I think Dad had light hair when he was a baby. You can ask Grandma when we get home."

She brushed Rosalie's hair away from her face. "The same thing will probably happen to you and Michael too. You're my Roe and I love you the whole world."

"I love you too Mommy. Did Aunt Lucille have blonde hair when she was little?"

Mom had a twin sister, but they were not identical twins. They were fraternal twins. Aunt Lucille's husband, Uncle Vezy said that mom and Aunt Lucille were the two most beautiful girls in school.

"No. Aunt Lucille was always dark, but we both had green eyes. We should call her when we get home. Speaking of green, let's get some trees. Do you see any you like?"

There were saplings all around them. Rosalie and Mom choose the ones they wanted and waited for Dad and Michael. They came toward them with shovels in their hands. Dad and Mom dug up 6 more trees. Mom and Dad each took two trees and Michael and Rosalie each carried one to the car. They put the trees in the trunk and drove back to their house with the smiling eyes.

It was hot, but Grandma Rosalie and Grandma Rose came outside with a tray of ice cold water. Michael and Rosalie sat on the slate steps and watched Dad and Mom digging holes around the side of the house and then in front of the house by the road. When they were done, Rosalie and Michael put their trees in the holes and helped pat the dirt down around the baby trees. They would grow to be the most beautiful and magnificent trees and a constant reminder of the day on de Vrie mountain.

THE DOLL HOUSE

After dinner, Mom started running the hot water and the sink filled up with white soapy suds. The kitchen was in the back of the house. It had a wooden door to the right that was mostly glass except for the bottom. There was a window with pretty curtains above the sink. The house used to end there until a back porch lined with windows was added. From the kitchen and through the porch you could see the circular garden, a lilac bush, the apple tree, and the Unadilla River down the hill.

Doing dishes was something Rosalie and Michael did together with Grandma Rosalie and Grandma Rose. Michael would clear the table bringing the dishes to the counter. Grandma Rosalie would wash the dishes, getting them all soapy, and hand them to Grandma Rose. Grandma Rose would rinse them off in very hot water and hand them to Rosalie. They were still hot when Rosalie dried them off and put them on the kitchen table. The hot wet glasses were stacked in the drying rack. Together they would put the dishes into the glass cabinets. Once the dishes were done and put away, they would head into the family room.

Living in the valley of South New Berlin, the reception was weak, so there was only one channel on the television, and getting it to come in clear took a little bit of work. Dad put the TV on channel 4 which was nothing but static and hints of voices. He headed outside to the big metal antenna attached to the side of the house. Grandma Rosalie and Grandma Rose sat in the two chairs on either side of the front door. Rosalie stood in the dining room. Michael stood in the kitchen in the doorway leading to the back porch. Mom stood in the doorway of the back porch leading outside.

Dad turned the antenna and asked Mom, "Is it good now?"

Mom asked Michael, "Is it good now?"

Michael asked Rosalie, "Is it good now?"

Rosalie asked the grandmas, "Is it good now?"

"No," said the grandmas.

"No," said Rosalie.

"No," said Michael.

"No," said Mom.

Dad turned the antenna a little bit more. "How about now?" he asked.

"How about now?" asked Mom.

"How about now?" asked Michael.

"How about now?" asked Rosalie.

From the family room the grandmas yelled, "IT'S GOOD!"

"IT'S GOOD," yelled Rosalie.

"IT'S GOOD," yelled Michael.

"IT'S GOOD," said Mom.

Dad came inside, washed his hands, and joined the family for whatever was on channel 4 that night. Sitting around the TV, the grandmas crocheted, Mom and Dad worked on a puzzle, and Rosalie and Michael sat on the floor. There on the television was the most beautiful dollhouse Rosalie had ever seen. She gasped. "Mom, look! Can I get that?"

Without looking up, hand on a puzzle piece, Mom said, "We'll talk about it tomorrow."

Tomorrow came and with it came Aage. He opened the side door and gave the bell a ping with his knuckle.

"Mornin!"

Rosalie and Michael came running down the stairs still in pajamas. They gave Aage a hug and headed straight into the kitchen for breakfast.

"Mom, can I get that dollhouse that I showed you yesterday? The one that was on the television?"

"Good morning," said Mom.

"Mom, the dollhouse. I really really really want it," Rosalie pleaded.

"Good morning," she said again. "Perhaps you could put that on your Christmas list," said Mom.

"But that's so far away," Rosalie said through a well up of tears and a quiver of her lip. She ran past Aage and headed up to her room. Ted was sitting on her bed. She picked him up. He understood everything without her having to say a word.

A few minutes later there was a knock on the door. It was Mom. She had a smile on her face. She was so beautiful. Rosalie was crying, holding Ted as Mom sat down next to her.

"I remember when I got Ted," Mom started. "I was about fifteen years old. He had a big red bow around his neck. I loved him so much, but when you were born, I put him in your crib with you. I want you to know how much it means to me that you love him as much as I did."

Rosalie listened while droplets of tears streamed down her face. Her mom was brushing the hair away from her face with her fingers and wiping tears off of her chin.

"I really want a dollhouse," she pleaded taking breaths in between each word.

"I know. Sometimes there are a lot of things we want, or we think we want. It's a good idea to write them down. When you look at that list in a few weeks, you may decide you want different things. And Roe, sometimes we just can't get everything we want. I love you. You know that?"

"Yes."

"Let's wash your face and then head downstairs. Do you want to make silver dollar pancakes with me? I'm sure Aage would like some," said Mom.

Rosalie gave Mom and hug and together they went downstairs. Rosalie's face was pink from rubbing tears from her eyes and cheeks. She saw Aage sitting at the dining room table with Dad.

"Hi Rosalie. Why so sad?" asked Aage. He spoke slowly, as if his words were on a Sunday walk through town.

Rosalie looked at Mom and Dad. "I want a dollhouse, but...." she looked at Mom again, "but," she almost started crying again, "but I have to wait."

Aage looked at her with his blue eyes and the corners of his mouth turned up. "I have to go," and just like that, he left.

"He didn't even get to have any pancakes," said Rosalie.

The morning turned into afternoon. Afternoon turned into evening. Evening turned into morning again. Just as he had done the day before, Aage Jensson came walking through the front door giving the bell a ping with his knuckle. Rosalie and Michael were in the kitchen having breakfast and got up to give him a hug.

"Good morning. I'm glad you're awake. Stay right here," and Aage left again.

He returned with a dollhouse. It was white with a green roof, just like their house. It had two big rooms on the first floor, a staircase, and two big rooms on the second floor. There were real windows and a big wooden door, just like their house. The windows had beautiful curtains and the rooms on the first floor had carpeting. Rosalie could not believe it. Aage made her a dollhouse.

"I spoke with your folks before bringing this over. My daughter Ann made the curtains. If you don't like them she has other fabric at home," said Aage.

"I love them. I love this house. And I love you Aage," said Rosalie.

Aage's dollhouse did not look like any dollhouse Rosalie had ever seen. You certainly couldn't buy something like it in a store. No, this was a country house. The second floor had ruler markings on it from the piece of wood Aage used. The carpeting was not dollhouse carpeting, but real carpeting. Rosalie loved it. Mom and Dad said they would get her furniture and a family for Christmas.

Michael was looking up at Aage wide-eyed. Aage picked up Michael and said, "Don't think I don't have something for you too," and he carried him outside. From the kitchen window Rosalie saw Aage put Michael down and open his car door. He knelt down and handed Michael a tin. Aage scooped Michael up and carried him back into the house. Once inside, he pried open the top of the tin. Inside were layers and layers of molasses cookies. Taped to the top of the inside of the tin was a note in perfect handwriting, "Rosalie and Michael, Nice meeting you. Sigrid."

As it turns out, Sigrid did in fact make the best molasses cookies.

GRANDMAS' PIZZA

Just like Aage's dollhouse was unlike any dollhouse you could buy, Grandma Rosalie and Grandma Rose made pizza you could only get at home. The grandmas were in the kitchen making dough for lunch. There was flour all over the kitchen table, all over their dresses, and all over their hands. Sitting at the table, they kneaded the dough, rolling it and turning it until it formed two big balls. They placed the balls of dough in greased bowls and covered them to let the dough rise.

"Michael, Rosalie? Can the two of you go into the backyard and pick some apples?" asked Grandma Rosalie.

Rosalie and Michael looked at each other and jumped up. Apples meant apple pie. They ran out the back door, around the circular garden, and down the hill to the apple tree. It grew perfectly for climbing. There were a lot of apples that had fallen to the ground so they put them into a bucket and brought them into the house through the back porch. Then they ran back outside. Rosalie shook the low branches while

Michael picked the apples off the ground as they fell.

Grandma Rose had just finished wiping down the kitchen table and was ready to start slicing apples. She and Grandma Rosalie had short knives, which they used to peel the apples. They did it with such precision that you could almost see through the skin as it fell off the apples.

Once all the apples were peeled, Grandma Rose would cut them in quarters and Grandma Rosalie would cut out the core. Rosalie and Michael were mesmerized. Every so often one of the grandmas would hand them each a piece of apple. To the bowl of apples Grandma Rosalie added cinnamon, nutmeg, ginger, sugar, and some cream of tartar. Then they piled the apples into a pie crust and covered them with small pieces of butter. Grandma Rose rolled out the top pie crust and then Grandma Rosalie sliced it into strips. Carefully they laid the strips over the heaping apples to create a lattice top. It was a work of art. Into the over the apple pie went. As it was cooking they took the bowls of pizza dough and removed the cloths that had been placed on top. Inside, the dough had grown twice its size. Each ball looked fluffy and airy.

Grandma Rose put her hand into a jar of flour and sprinkled it onto the kitchen table like she was feeding chickens. She put her bowl on the kitchen table, flipped it over and the dough ball landed in the pile of flour. It made a cloud a smoke, like mist in the morning covering the grass. They kneaded that dough over and over again. Rosalie and Michael were given their own balls of dough to knead. The dough was soft and felt smooth covered in flour. When the grandmas said it was time, they started making small pizzas, no bigger than a saucer for a teacup. The entire table was covered with round discs of dough glistening under the florescent lights of the kitchen. Grandma

115

Rose pulled baking sheets out from under the oven and Grandma Rosalie greased them lightly with a paper towel dipped in olive oil. Together they placed the round pizzas onto the baking sheets. Grandma Rose handed Rosalie a spoon and together they covered each pizza dough with sauce. Grandma Rosalie placed a piece of fresh basil in the center of each pie and Michael covered the basil and sauce with a handful of mozzarella cheese.

Bzzzzzzzzz. The oven timer went off. Grandma Rose opened the oven door and a wave of heat came pouring out onto Rosalie and Michael sitting at the kitchen table. The apple pie was done. The smell of cinnamon and apples filled the kitchen and overtook the freshly made pizza still sitting on the table. As Grandma Rose put the apple pie on the stovetop, Grandma Rosalie picked up the baking sheets filled with pizza and put them into the hot oven. While the pizza cooked, the grandmas cleaned the stove top and set the table. When the timer went off, Mom and Dad came into the kitchen. Grandma Rosalie took the pizza out of the oven while Grandma Rose filled everyone's glass with water.

Michael sat on the side of the kitchen table by the cabinets with Grandma Rose.

Rosalie sat on the other side of the kitchen table by the refrigerator and oven next to Grandma Rosalie. The pizza was amazing. You couldn't get anything like this from a restaurant. The crust was soft on the inside but crispy on the outside. The cheese was melted and browned from the broiler. Rosalie took the big piece of basil off of her pizza. Grandma Rosalie ate it. Rosalie loved sitting next to Grandma Rosalie. She always ate whatever Rosalie did not like. She was good like that.

After lunch, Dad asked Michael to get him an apple. This was an exciting part of lunch and dinner time.

Dad would hold the apple in his left hand. With a sharp knife in his right hand, he would peel the apple slowly, going around and around the apple, without the skin breaking. Sometime it would look at though the skin was going to fall, but Dad kept it all together. Then he would put the apple down and with his two hands he would re-shape the skin into an apple, as if it was still there in the middle. It was like putting a puzzle together. Dad would cut the apple up and give everyone a slice. He did this with fruit at almost every meal.

They let the pie cool and enjoyed it later that night after dinner. The grandmas made delicious pies and their crusts were the best.

THE BROKEN GLASS

After lunch one sunny day, Michael cleared the table and Grandma Rose filled the kitchen sink with hot soapy water. Michael then headed outside with Grandma Rosalie to finish hanging laundry with Mom. In the kitchen, it was just Rosalie and Grandma Rose.

Grandma would wash the dishes and Rosalie would dry them. Grandma Rose handed Rosalie a glass and she thought she had it, but CRASH. It hit the floor and shattered into several pieces. Rosalie gasped and tears appeared out of the corners of her eyes.

She was frightened by the sound and embarrassed. Grandma Rose knelt down and picked up the broken pieces and placed them on the kitchen counter.

"Why is my girl so sad?" she asked.

"I can't believe I broke the glass. What if we can't do the dishes together anymore?"

Grandma Rose kissed her and gave her a hug. She took Rosalie's hand, put the broken glass in the front pocket of her house dress, and said, "Come with me."

Mom walked in and said, "Where are you two going?" and Grandma replied, "For a walk."

Out the door they went. Mom was watching from the kitchen window. They walked down the steps, around the front of the house to the circular drive, and down the pebble covered driveway. When they got to the road, Grandma turned left toward the de Vrie's house.

Grandma's hand was soft and warm. Together they walked along the side of the road. The sun's rays heated their faces. Then Grandma stopped. She put her hand in her pocket, took the broken glass pieces out, and threw them into the grassy field.

"There. All gone," she said with her tender and loving voice.

Rosalie was shocked. Grandma just threw the broken glass into the field. She looked up at Grandma who was smiling down at her.

Nobody ever found out about the broken glass. Nobody, except Mom who was watching from the house, head tilted, with a smile on her face.

PAJAMA PILLOW

Night time at the summer house was magical. There was a peace that fell over the house. Walking outside and looking up felt like living in the center of a snow globe. There were stars everywhere lighting up the midnight sky. There were no buildings, no cars, no billboards, nothing for the eyes to see other than the shadows of mountains and the dark night lit up under a dome of stars.

Some nights Rosalie, Michael, Mom, Dad, and the grandmas would play cards. One of their favorite card games was Spite and Malice, which Mrs. de Vrie taught them. Other nights they would do a big puzzle together. Michael would put in the last piece.

Tonight the entire family was watching television and Grandma Rosalie was teaching Rosalie how to needlepoint. Nestled between her two grandmas, Rosalie held a teddy bear needlepoint canvas. Grandma said once it was completed she would make it into a pillow for Rosalie's bed. Each grandma was crocheting a blanket while watching Rosalie's stitches at the same time. Every now and then they would tell her to pull the yarn a little tighter to make her stitches even. Other times they would tell her to redo a section, which Rosalie dreaded.

Night after night sitting between her grandmas, Rosalie put the needle through the canvas and carefully pulled it up. Up and down, up and down she completed color after color. Grandma Rose would finish each section off, cut the yarn, and then go back to her own crocheting. Finally Rosalie just had the background to complete. She worked the cream yarn through the canvas, up in one hole, down into the next, up in one hole, down into the next, up, down, up, down, until finally she was done.

Admiring her work, Rosalie laid the finished needlepoint on her lap and ran her hands across it. It was soft. Then she stood up and a terrible thing happened. The needlepoint stayed on her nightgown. Rosalie had sewn her needlepoint onto her pajamas. She sighed and dropped her head, looking down at her dangling canvas. All of her hard work would have to be taken out and done over. Grandma Rosalie looked at the needlepoint hanging from the nightgown and a smile appeared on her face.

"I have an idea," said Grandma. She continued, "Rose, give me your scissors."

Grandma Rose reached into her crochet bag filled with yarn and pulled out small metal scissors.

"Stay still. I'm going to cut your needlepoint off of the nightgown," said Grandma Rosalie.

With eyes wide open, Rosalie watched as one grandma held her needlepoint and the other one cut the nightgown. Rosalie had a big hole where her nightgown used to be. You could see her legs and knees. Rosalie started laughing and looked at Mom and Dad. They were laughing too.

"I guess we'll get you some new pajamas tomorrow. Michael, would you like some new pajamas too?" asked Mom.

Grandma Rosalie got up and went to her room. She returned with a pink pillow, just about the same size as Rosalie's needlepoint. She looked at Rosalie and asked, "What do you think?"

"It's perfect!"

Grandma Rose held the pillow while Grandma Rosalie trimmed back the nightgown with her scissors. Then she folded the sides of the needlepoint in and placed it on the pillow the make sure it fit perfectly. Grandma Rose held it in place while Grandma Rosalie threaded her needle. Carefully, and without sewing it onto her own house dress, Grandma sewed the teddy bear needlepoint onto the pink velvet like pillow. It looked beautiful. She handed it to Rosalie who gave both grandmas big hugs.

"That is just beautiful! We're so proud of you. It's late though. Time for a story and prayers," said Mom and Dad.

Rosalie and Michael said goodnight to Grandma Rose and Grandma Rosalie, giving them both a kiss and a hug. Walking upstairs Rosalie held her pillow in her arms. This pillow was for Ted.

That night after Mom and Dad had tucked them in, Rosalie looked over and saw Ted's head on his own pillow, a pillow she made just for him. She put her arm around him and brushed the wall with her hand.

"Good night, Ted. With God all things are possible."

END OF SUMMER

That first summer in New York State, the days were filled with walks to town in the little red wagon lined with pillows, Toby rocking in his rocking chair, and ice cream at Madison's. It was about walking through the bees ever so slowly, stopping in for a visit with Aage and Sigrid Jensson, Mrs. Bibble, and the de Vries, gardening, and playing on the tire swing. This summer memories were made fishing at the Barr-Y with no bait, candy from the Snack Bar, running through the sprinkler, horseback riding, walks up de Vrie mountain, the

Grandmas nestled on the couch crocheting watching channel 4 on the television, baking cookies, making puzzles, catching fireflies, church on Sundays, and having neighbors over who were now friends.

The summer was coming to an end. Dad took the Grandmas home and returned on Thursday. It was Labor Day weekend. On Saturday, Mom took the clothes line down and stored it in the tool shed. Dad watered the garden one last time. Rosalie and Michael packed up their clothes in garbage bags and brought them downstairs. That night, all the neighbors came over. Mrs. Bibble brought her husband Don and a jar full of honey. All of the de Vries came by with two loaves of zucchini bread. Mr. and Mrs. Jensson were there too. The adults stayed in the kitchen and dining room laughing and talking, while the children played on the floor of the family room. As the night faded, one by one, everyone gathered by the front door. It was time to go. Michael stood in front of dad, and by his side was Rosalie, who stood in front of Mom.

Aage knelt down and said good-bye. He put his hand out to shake Rosalie's hand, but she threw herself in his arms and began to cry. "I'll miss you, Aage."

Michael started crying too, but Aage put his hands on Michael's chin, lifted his head, and then ruffled his hair. Bags of vegetables were on the front porch for everyone to take home. Mom and Dad told the neighbors they could pick whatever they wanted after they left. The garden was still in full bloom and vegetables would continue to grow throughout September.

The house seemed quiet and a little sad. Upstairs, Michael and Rosalie sat on the bed as Mom and Dad read them a story together. They talked about their summer and the school year ahead. It was getting late and Michael yawned. The family knelt by the bed under the moonlit night and said prayers in the summer house one final time. As Dad turned off the light they heard him say, "With God all things are possible."

After church on that warm Sunday morning, Mom made peanut butter and jelly sandwiches and carefully stacked them in the plastic bread bag. She brought the little red wagon into the tool shed and locked it up. Dad told Rosalie and Michael to use the bathroom before going down to the basement to turn the water off. Mom set the heat to 55 degrees so the pipes wouldn't freeze during the harsh winter months.

In her room, Rosalie carved a tiny cross in the closet using the key from the front door. All the windows were closed and all that remained was Ted on her bed. She picked him up and headed downstairs, placing the key in the door again. Mom turned all the lights off and they all said good-bye to their house. On the way out the white wooden door with the big glass window, Dad lifted Michael up to ring the bell on final time. He turned and locked the house up with the big iron key.

They stopped by the de Vries with whatever food was left in the refrigerator and said their goodbyes. The de Vries were wonderful neighbors who said they would watch over the house. Dad pulled out of the de Vrie driveway and headed back to the summer house one last time.

"It was a good summer. I love you all so much. Let's get one last picture in front of our house."

They got out of the car and Dad took a picture of Rosalie and Michael sitting on the slate porch. Rosalie took a picture of Mom and Dad, their arms around each other.

Riding down the road on bicycles was Ana and Finn. Ana was waving her arms, signaling for them to wait. The pulled into the driveway leaving their bikes lifeless on the grass. Out of breath, Ana handed Rosalie a piece of paper. It was her address.

"Write to me every week and I'll write back, okay?"

She gave Ana a big hug and told her she'd see her for Thanksgiving. Dad asked Ana to take a picture of them standing outside the house with the smiling eyes.

It was sunny and their eyes were squinting as they looked at the camera. Dad was standing next to Mom, his hand draped over her shoulder. Rosalie and Michael were standing in front of them. They were country folk now and the summer house was part of them with its garden, apple tree, and circular driveway lined with painted white rocks. Rosalie thought maybe she was always a country girl. She just needed her summer house to show her the way. Ana took one final picture.

Mom put Michael in the car and then got in herself. Rosalie sat next to Michael with Ted on her lap. Dad turned the key to start the car, shifted into gear, and slowly pulled away. From the window they watched Ana and Finn waving goodbye.

With Ted in her arms they drove around the bend, through the bees, and past the Bibble's house on the right. Dad tooted the horn.

Down the long road they continued and drove past the Barr-Y on the left. The horses were outside swishing their tails. Their heads were buried in the grass. As they continued they came to Aage's house. Mom rolled down the window and waved to Mr. and Mrs. Jensson sitting outside on their porch. Again, Dad tooted the horn.

They turned onto Route 23 and smiled when they saw Toby sitting in his rocking chair outside Toby's Antiques. They passed the back of the sign that read, "Welcome to South New Berlin."

The road was quiet. Up and down the hills they went, around the bends, and along the Unadilla River. After a half hour, Dad asked Mom for a peanut butter and jelly sandwich. Rosalie fell asleep somewhere along Route 17 with Ted in her arms and Ana's address in her hand. She dreamed of her red and white summer house with the smiling eyes, her bed under the window, and the love of her family.

From the front seat she heard her Mom say, "Michael and Rosalie, I love you the whole world."

Dad took Mom's hand. "The most important things are in that back seat. With God all things are possible."

GOOD NEWS BAD NEWS

School started. The weather turned cooler and the leaves had changed. Green leaves turned to hues of red, orange, and yellow. Autumn was Rosalie's favorite time of year. Then autumn began to disappear as Thanksgiving approached. The vibrant colors of the fall began to turn brown and grey. Back in Brooklyn, Rosalie had been writing letters to Ana every week. Mom bought Rosalie new stationary and she would always put some aside for Ana. They wrote about school, funny stories, trading stationary when they were together again, and how much they missed each other. Rosalie was excited about going back upstate for Thanksgiving. However, that would not happen.

Mom and Dad walked into the family room where Rosalie and Michael were playing. They asked Rosalie and Michael to come up off the floor and sit with them on the couch. It sounded serious.

"We have some good news and some bad news," said Dad. He was looking at Mom.

Rosalie looked at Michael. This didn't sound good. They looked at Dad. He took Mom's hand.

Mom added, "We won't be going upstate for Thanksgiving as planned. We're very sorry."

Michael's jaw dropped open. Rosalie was visibly disappointed and asked, "Why?"

"Wait, wait, now. Before you get upset we have some good news too. Actually, it is wonderful news. We have something for you," Dad said stretching out his hands.

He handed Rosalie two small figures and placed two larger figures in Michael's hands.

"What's this?" asked Michael.

"It's a family. Actually, our family for the doll house that Aage made," explained Mom.

Inside Michael's hands was a Mom and Dad. Inside Rosalie's hands was a girl and a boy. And then Dad held up another doll wrapped up in a blanket.

"Mom's having a baby," said Dad and then he smiled and looked at Mom.

"I'm having a baby," continued Mom, putting her hands on her stomach, moving them up and down. "That's why we cannot go upstate."

Rosalie put her hands to her mouth. She wanted to scream with joy, but didn't know if it would make the baby in Mom's belly cry. Michael walked up to Mom and asked, "There's a baby in there?"

"Yes. It's your baby brother or sister. What do you think, Michael? Would you like a little brother or sister?" asked Mom.

"I'd like a pony," said Michael. Everyone started laughing.

On June 25, baby Andréa was born. Michael and Rosalie were home with Grandma Rosalie when the call came in.

"It's a GIRL! It's a GIRL!" Grandma yelled with joy. Rosalie and Michael hugged each other jumping up and down. Dad said the baby weighed 8 pounds 4 ounces and had lots of dark hair. They decided to name her after Dad's dad, Grandpa Andréa. Mom and Dad came home from the hospital with their new sister and Andréa was beautiful.

Two weeks later, Dad and Mom packed up everyone's clothes in plastic bags. While Dad packed the car, Rosalie and Michael made peanut butter and jelly sandwiches, put them in plastic bags, and then back into the bread sleeve. They wouldn't be coming back to Brooklyn until Labor Day. Rosalie went upstairs to her room just like she did the summer before, although this time there was a crib in her room. Using her finger she etched a cross in the carpeting in her closet. She took Ted, and hopped into the back seat of the car with Michael and Andréa. They rolled out of their driveway and were on the road. A half hour into the drive Dad asked for a sandwich and some pretzels. With the hum of the road beneath her feet, Rosalie dozed off. Ted feel asleep too.

They woke up as they came to South New Berlin. Toby was sitting outside in his old rocking chair as if he had never moved. They made a right at Madison's and headed across the bridge over the Unadilla River. When the got to the yellow house, they made a left onto their road. As they passed Aage's house Dad tooted the horn. Smoke and kicked up dirt consumed the road behind them. As they passed the Bibble's Bee Farm on the left, Dad tooted the horn.

The red barn with the large doors was around a bend. They were nearly home.

Rosalie lifted Ted. The car slowed as they approached the green garage. Dad turned on the signal to make a left into the circular driveway and came to a stop in front of their house with the smiling eyebrows.

"We're home," said Dad.

"We're home," confirmed Mom. "I love you, Dom. Thank you for doing all the driving."

"I'll unpack," he said. "You bring the kids inside. Hey, Lillian," Dad paused and waited for her to look at him. He smiled and said, "With God all things are possible."

Aage's Dollhouse

Inside Aage's Dollhouse

Ted and the Pajama Pillow

Rosalie Intartaglia spent summers in upstate New York with her family. Many years later her children spent their summers at the same home in South New Berlin. Rosalie, her husband, and children still enjoy going to New York State each summer. Mom and Dad recently built a new summer house upstate where the family still gathers today. The summer house in South New Berlin was home to the Intartaglia family for more than forty years. Rosalie wrote this book for her children Olivia and Dominick, and Andréa's children Nora and Lily. Rosalie's second book in the Summer House series is set to be published in 2019. There are so many more memories to share.